The Starlover Series Book 1:

Project Earth

Ali Noel Vyain

This is a work of fiction. Names, characters, places, and incidents either are the product of the author's imagination or are used fictitiously. Any resemblance to actual persons, living or dead, events, or locales is entirely coincidental.

Copyright © 2018 by Ali Noel Vyain.

Published by Ali Noel Vyain at Smashwords.

No part of this book can be reproduced or used in any manner without written permission of the copyright owner.

Elsewhere

eISBN: 9781370189458

print ISBN: 9798201635831

1st edition printing

alinoelvyain.wordpress.com

Also By Ali Noel Vyain

The Colonies of Earth Series
The Colonies of Earth (Eris): Different
The Colonies of Earth (Venus): In Men's Shadows
The Colonies of Earth Series: Tales From Mars
The Colonies of Earth: The Colonies Will Be Independent
The Colonies of Earth: (Orcus): The Amazons Rise Up
The Colonies of Earth (Pluto): First Time
The Colonies of Earth (Saturn & Titan): Praying for Death
The Colonies of Earth (Mercury): This Strange, Wild Land
The Colonies of Earth (The Moon): The Crossroads
The Colonies of Earth (Triton): The Mistress
The Colonies of Earth (Neptune): The Plantation Owner
The Colonies of Earth (Ceres): The Vampire's Girlfriend
The Colonies of Earth (Titania): Vampire Struggles
The Colonies of Earth (Haumea): Aftermath
The Colonies of Earth: Box Set

The Starlover Series
Book 1: Project Earth
Book 2: Uncle & Niece
Book 3: Traveling Teenager
Book 4: Cassandra the Red Tiger
The Starlover Series Box Set

The Violet Series

The Guardian Series

Sir Socks Le Chat
The Life Adventures of Sir Socks Le Chat
The Diary of Sir Socks Le Chat
The Afterlife Adventures of Sir Socks Le Chat
Sir Socks Le Chat (a box set)

Poetry
Scientist in Training Gone Mad
Honoring the Cats in My Life
Thoughts on Turning 40
Transitions
Unexpected
By Accident of Birth
Failure
Mental Illness
Insanity
In the Name of Survival
Food or Poison
Myths
Becoming a Black Unicorn
All About Cats
Medusa
Night Hags
The Desert
Content Creator

Non-Fiction Books

Contents

Chapter | Two Brothers

Frederick and David Mueller stood at the pair of open caskets. In one was their mother. In the other was their father. It was a shuttle accident that no one could have foreseen. Here were the results. At least two dead on impact. Now these two young, barely men were orphans.

It was a good thing they were close. Or else they might not have survived the impact of their parents' deaths.

"Mom? Dad? I hope you're comfortable. Fred and I are here. We came to say our final goodbye."

"Goodbye."

"Goodbye, Mom and Dad. We're be fine. Just have a little faith in both of us." Dave nodded to Fred.

They turned away from the coffins and stood around to wait for others to come to the funeral. Many people came and went to give condolences. Some stayed for the funeral service. Fred sighed. It was too long for him to be in a monkey suit. But the service wasn't over. They still had to go to the graveyard.

The two brothers went together. They stood side by side as they watched the coffins lowered into the same grave plot. By that time, no one was talking. The coffins were at least six feet under and safe from anything causing any problems. The equipment was removed and soon people left the graveyard.

There were no more words. The depth of despair was great for the brothers, but yet they still were looking forward to living their lives.

"Ready to go?" asked Dave.

"Yes," said Fred.

They turned and left the graveyard. Dave flew their shuttle back to the family home. Along the way Fred took off his tie. The brothers didn't speak. Fred thought about their shared childhood. He was the younger brother. The second son. Their parents had considered him second best.

It was not a pleasant situation to say the least. Dave was the one who did better in school. Fred wasn't always interested. Unless he was building things. It didn't matter if the building materials were legos or electronics. He just wanted to build.

Dave was the intelligent scientific brother who loved to research. He like to come up with hypotheses and test them rigorously as he could. Fred kept building. He had learned how to repair things which would break down around the house. He could even repair the computers. He willingly fixed anything that had broken in the house. It was something he had never grown out of.

But his parents had thought it was beneath his station in life. "Freddie, why can't you be a scientist like your brother?"

"I'm not interested. I just want to build and fix things."

"But repair work isn't a good profession."

"Why not?"

"Only stupid people do that sort of work."

"What? Are you sure? Tradespeople can earn decent money even by your standards."

"But only stupid people do that sort of work. Why can't you be more like your brother?"

"If tradespeople are so stupid, why is it that electricians have to use trigonometry in their work?"

"What? That can't be true."

"It is. I took the classes, so I would know."

That had kept their parents quiet for several days.

Dave had gone on to college and had studied hard. He had found some work in research at his school and had done well with it. He had graduated with honors. Their parents had been thrilled.

"Freddie, when are you going to go to college?"

"And do what there?"

"Get a degree like your brother has. We are proud that he will become one of the best scientists Earth has ever had."

"Good for him."

"Freddie! What are you going to do with your life?"

He had simply shrugged his shoulders. "I'm happy repairing things that break down around here and doing repair work for others. I earn some money that way. What's the big deal?"

"You're too much of a dreamer. Someday you will have to grow up."

Fred had smiled at his parents. At least they had a united front. "Look, I'm not interested in what Dave is interested in enough to do what he does. I like what I do. I'm still building things in my spare time, as I'm sure you've noticed. I'm using those scrap parts that no one cares about. Doesn't that mean anything to you?"

"It's a terrible hobby. Inventors don't earn as much as scientists."

Fred had sighed. "We're getting nowhere. Clearly you can appreciate the money I've saved you over the years. I'd say it's helped with my upkeep."

His parents had kept quiet for a few more days. Actually, it was the last time Fred had talked to them. The shuttle accident had happened soon after. Now he was without them.

The brothers were home. They went to the living room and sat down on different chairs. Dave sighed. He leaned back in his chair.

"What are we going to do, Fred?"

"About what?"

"About the house. About their things."

"Oh, I hadn't thought about it."

"Well, we need to do something. I doubt we could afford to maintain this place."

"I can do the repairs as I have for a long time."

Dave smiled. "I know that. But there are utilities. And we

still need to eat."

"Oh. Is the house paid off?"

"Yeah, but there are property taxes to pay."

"Oh, right. You don't technically have a job right now."

"No, I don't. I know you earn some money repairing things for other people. And that's good. That will help. But we have to deal with the house."

"Perhaps we should sell it and most of the things here?"

Dave sat up. "What are you thinking?"

"If we can't afford it, then we shouldn't try to hang on to everything. Perhaps we need to let go and get a smaller place together."

"That sounds reasonable. I'm glad you can still think." He paused. "Are you still upset that they wanted you to be like me?"

"Yeah, but they're dead now. What can they say to me?"

Dave laughed. "Nothing. At least you're working. I'm the one who needs to find work."

Fred laughed with his brother. Later that evening they begun working on selling the house and most of the things in it. It had taken time, but they both had plenty of that now that neither one was in school or had regular jobs.

Chapter 2 Project Earth

"Fred, what are you going to do with your life?" asked Dave.

"Oh? I want to build a spaceship."

"You were always a dreamer."

"Dreams are just the beginning."

Dave chuckled. "Well, I'm going to start a research project."

"Oh?"

"I'm calling it Project Earth. I want to find ways we can save the planet before we completely destroy it."

Fred smiled. "Way to go. So, is this for a major research university?"

"Well, no. It's privately funded. I sent out project proposals and got the money. Now it's a matter of getting more scientists and their families to join in the project."

"Wonderful. I am happy for you."

"You are welcome to come with me."

"Thanks. I think I will. You'll probably need someone to do repair work."

"Or help with the building."

"Yeah, that too."

"I'll make sure you'll be able to build your spaceship."

"Mom and Dad would never approve of me doing this."

"I know. But I'm your brother and I know how happy it makes you to experiment with building and doing repair work."

Fred smiled. "So, where will you be working on Project Earth?"

"In Transylvania."

"Whoa! Are the stories true that come from there? You know, about Dracula?"

"Well, they are at least based on some facts. There was a count Dracula who had a tendency to set out the bodies of his enemies completely drained of blood."

"Eww."

"Yeah, I know. But that's as far as it goes."

"I see. When do we leave?"

"We can leave as soon as the house and what we're not taking is turned over."

"So we better pack now."

"Good idea."

They started packing. It seemed to take them a long time. But they were done before the estate sellers showed up.

"Ah, so your bags aren't a part of the sale?" asked the seller.

"That is correct," answered Dave. "We'll be staying at a local hotel while the sale is on."

"That will make things easier. I've already made the announcements. I'm sure there will be plenty of people who will stop by." She checked her notes. "Oh, I see that the house is to be sold as well."

"Yes. I hope that's not a problem."

"Oh, no, not at all. We can handle that too. I will contact you that same day after the sale is over to let you know what sold and what didn't."

"Do you think everything will sell?"

"Probably. Usually we can sell everything or most everything. It just depends upon what's here and what people are interested in."

"Okay. Good luck with the sale."

"Why thank you. It is a lot of hard work, but not impossible. You two go off and have some fun. I've got everything under control here."

The two brothers took their bags and walked to the shuttle. Dave flew it to a hotel they both knew and had always liked. They got to the hotel and checked into one room with two beds. They got inside and set their bags down.

Fred laid down on one of the beds. Dave sighed.

"You have any ideas on what we could do while we wait?" asked Dave.

"We could go to the bar and see what women we can pick up."

Dave smiled and shook his head. "You are such a playboy."

Fred smiled. "I know. Perhaps you should try it sometime."

"Hmm. I don't know. I'd worry about STDs and getting a girl pregnant."

"I have plenty of condoms. They work well enough."

"Well, maybe."

"Or would you prefer to find a girlfriend?"

"That actually sounds better to me."

"To each his own."

They went to a bar. They flirted. They danced. But they didn't take anyone back to their hotel room that night. Instead, they went back to their room alone. They made it in time to get the video call from the estate sales agent.

"Oh, there you are, boys! I have excellent news. Everything including the house sold. So, now all you have to do is stop by tomorrow and we'll finish up all the paperwork. You don't need to go to the closing for the house. Just stop by my office in the morning."

"Sure thing. We'll be there."

They cut the connection. Dave looked at Fred.

"Well, that's almost done. We can leave from the office to Transylvania when we're done there."

"Good idea. We'll check out before we leave to finish up that paperwork."

"Why do we still call it paperwork? We do use any real paper anymore."

Fred laughed.

The next day, they wasted no time getting ready in the morn-ing. They packed their bags and put them in the shuttle. They checked out. Soon they were on board the shuttle heading towards the office. The virtual paperwork didn't take too much time. The brothers both got 50 percent each delivered to their separate accounts. They confirmed the new account balances. They shook hands with the estate sales agent and left her office.

They were in the shuttle when they both received messages that the funds wouldn't be available until next week.

Dave sighed. Fred shrugged his shoulders.

"Dave, we should be fine for another week. We have enough money to get us to Transylvania. We won't go hungry. We'll have what we need until the money becomes available."

"You're right. I'm sure we'll be fine. I'm just nervous."

"It's understandable. I think it's scary, but I looked over our finances before we got these messages. I knew we'd be okay for longer than a week."

Dave smiled. "Alright, let's go to Transylvania. Although we should get fuel before we actually take off."

"We can get food too. Then we won't have to make any stops."

"Alright."

They stopped at a fuel station. Filled up the shuttle's tank. Stocked up on snack food. Plenty of snack food. It was going to be a long trip and they tended to get quite hungry. They loaded up the shuttle and planned their flight path to their destination. They were to land near the famous Dracula's castle.

Dave had to set the computer to automatic so that he and

Fred could sleep when they needed to. The computer would alert them if there was a problem in the flight pattern. There were no problems. The flight was uneventful besides their reminiscing, eating, and napping. They enjoyed themselves one last time before Dave and Fred would get engrossed in their projects.

Fred's would get delayed due to lack of money for another week. But he would find it wouldn't be a problem. In fact as soon as the two brothers arrived at the site, they were greeted by Dr. Asimov and his assistant Hal.

"Welcome, David and Frederick Mueller. We've been waiting to meet you as soon as we heard about the project."

"You can call me, Dave."

"Dave, it is then. You're the one who came up with the idea for Project Earth. So what will you be doing, Frederick?"

"You can call me, Fred. I'll be on hand for any repair work. I hear there might be some building for me to do. But mainly I'll be building my own spaceship."

Dr. Asimov smiled. "I knew there was a reason I came here. Hal and I could help you with that project."

"Thanks. I'm still reading up on what I'll need for parts and deciding what I want it to be like."

"Wonderful. And Dave, don't feel left out. We'll be busy enough trying to think up and implementing good and safe ways to save this beautiful planet of ours."

Dave smiled. "It's okay. This is the first time anyone has recognized something my brother was doing. Our parents wanted him to be more like me."

"Well, they aren't here."

"No, they are no longer with us."

"I'm sorry to hear that."

"But we are looking forward to our projects."

"Good. Let's get you boys settled into your new home."

Chapter 3 Starlover

"Oh, there you are, Fred."

Fred turned to see his brother. "What's up, Dave?"

"I stopped by to see how your project is going."

"Oh, I'm still gathering parts."

"I have a few for you. We can't use these, but I thought you might be able to use them for something. They're still good."

"Thanks."

"Dr. Asimov is asking about you again. He's such a strange old guy."

"He's just as impressed by you and your ideas as he is by me. Relax."

Dave smiled. "I think I'm beginning to see what it was like for you growing up with our parents."

"Yeah?"

"Yeah, I don't think that was easy for you."

"It wasn't. We had a difference of opinion on what I should do with my life."

"They took it for granted that you did all the repair you did for all of us."

"And did you take it for granted?"

"No, you helped me when my microscope broke and you saved us all thousands of dollars. Easily. Or the time when my telescope fell apart. You just took some of the parts and some other scrap ones and built me another one. It worked just as well as the one that broke."

"I didn't mind doing any of that. I was glad that I could fix your things and you could get back to your work. I couldn't understand exactly what you were doing, but I knew you were happy to do it. I thought if I could fix those things or build you a new telescope, that we didn't need to spend the money that our parents complained was so scarce."

"And you were happy working like that. I just don't understand why it was such a big deal to them."

"They said it was beneath me. They wanted me to earn more money. They looked down on tradespeople."

"Tradespeople?"

"Yeah, I told them tradespeople could earn decent money by their standards. They couldn't believe I said that to them."

"It's true. They can earn good money. I think they have a different sort of intelligence from what I have."

"I pointed out to them that electricians had to use trigonometry. They were shocked."

"I didn't know that."

"You didn't take the classes."

"True. You did and you must be able to use it. We've never had an electrical problem with you on the job."

The brothers laughed.

"So, you'll talk to Dr. Asimov after dinner?"

"Yeah, why not? He does give me some good tips whenever I get stuck on my project."

"He's an excellent contributor on my project as well. I'm glad he's here."

"Even if he's strange."

"Yeah, even though he's strange."

After dinner, Dr. Asimov pulled Fred aside. The older man invited the younger one into his home. Hal followed them inside.

"How's your spaceship coming?"

"Oh, it's coming along nicely. I've been building four different faster than light speed drives for it."

"Wow! All four of them?"

"Yes. Warp drive, hyperdrive, the Heinlein Irrelevancy Drive, and the Adams Improbability Drive. I'd like to have all four in case one breaks down."

"Good thinking. I wonder why most shipbuilders don't think of such things."

"Probably the expense."

"Oh, is this project getting too expensive for you?"

"No. Well, not yet it isn't. I'm still using mostly scrap and spare parts that no one needs or wants anymore. Those do help."

"But will they need to be replaced sooner rather than later?"

"I don't know yet. My projects usually hold together fairly well."

"Yes, Dave has told me about a few of the things you've done for him over the years."

Fred smiled. "Some of which would have costs our parents thousands if I didn't do it."

"Yes, he mentioned that." Dr. Asimov paused. "I wanted to show you something. Perhaps you won't need it with your project, but I wanted to share it with you." He grabbed some sketches and his tablet computer. "Here, look these over and tell me what you think."

Fred looked at the sketches and the diagrams on the tablet. "Whoa!" He looked harder at the little details. "I can't believe it! I mean, I hope it's true. But we humans have tried and failed for years to design actual androids. I know there are robots, but none of them are this sophisticated."

"Then you understand why I have to keep this a secret?"

Fred looked up at Dr. Asimov. "A secret?"

"Yeah, people would be all over it. Probably wanting to lynch me or the android."

"Oh, right." Fred paused to look at Hal. "Did you actually make an android?"

Dr. Asimov smiled and said nothing.

"Oh, I see. You can't tell me if you did."

"That's right I can't answer that question."

"Okay. Well, thanks for showing me what you did. I'm fascinated, but I need to finish my spaceship."

"Have you named your ship?"

"Yes. It's *Starlover*."

"You must want to travel in space pretty badly."

"Yeah, I do."

"I'm sure you could build a robot to help you out on your spaceship easily. You're such a genius. I hope you know that."

Fred shrugged. "I'm just doing what I love, while I support my brother doing what he loves. I don't want more than that out of my life."

"Consider yourself lucky. Many people haven't always had a chance to do what they love in the name of survival."

Chapter 4 A Woman

The scientists were busy researching and Fred was busying building his spaceship. They tended to have mealtimes together. Someone would ring a bell to signal when the food was ready. Today was no exception. Someone rang the bell and everyone came together to eat.

But this mealtime was different. No one had any warning. Some of the greenery around them was moving without any benefit of the wind. They sat down and filled their plates with the food that was on the table. The greenery appeared to be moving closer to them. There was a brief pause in the meal. Some people shook their heads. Everyone resumed eating.

Without any warning, the greenery morphed into humanoid figures. They had green skin, green hair, and green eyes. There were men and women looking right at everyone eating their meal. By the time the green people appeared, everyone had stopped eating to stare back at them.

No one said anything for several minutes. No one knew what to say or do. No one was sure who the green skinned people were. Except for Dr. Asimov and Hal, no one could even guess what they were or why they were colored so green.

After several minutes, Hal broke the silence. "Welcome. I doubt that anyone here has ever met anyone like you before. But if I were to take a guess, I'd say you were earth nymphs."

Several green people smiled. "Yes, we are," one of them answered. "We've been watching you for quite some time. We noticed you were looking for ways to live without harming the planet. We'd like to contribute as well."

"We'd appreciate all the help we can get," Hal continued. "Many of us are new to some of these ways we've been trying out. Some of which were what our ancestors had done and were fine. I'm sure your input will be invaluable. As earth nymphs you must have a strong connection to the Earth."

"We do," several answered. Many just nodded their heads.

"We could use all the feedback we can get from the planet."

"That we can give. We can start with what you're eating."

"Oh, that doesn't affect anything," said someone.

"But it does. How you grow plants and how you treat animals greatly impacts the planet. Haven't any of learned what the biggest cause of global climate change is?"

No one answered.

"It was all the animals you killed for food. You did it on such a large scale that you wrecked the health of the planet and your own health as well. Animal products aren't necessarily better either. Many of you had to become vegan to save the planet before it was too late. That's why we want to start with food."

Dr. Asimov spoke up, "Very good. That was also my suggestion, but many of us still wanted to eat meat for some reason. I tried to explain that our biology doesn't require that we eat animal and animal products to get the right kind and the right amount of protein. We should be able to be vegans without too much trouble." He paused. "However, I am well aware that some may be experiencing cravings for meat. That should be addressed. I have some ideas on what we can offer as substitutes. I would recommend that you eat smaller portions until you don't have the cravings anymore."

"Alright, if it's for the project, then I'll try it, but I may not like the dietary changes."

"That's quite understandable. There are theories which suggest we learned to eat animals because it was too cold for the plants to grow and we needed to eat something. Hunger is quite an incentive."

They resumed their meal and offered some food to the earth nymphs. No one complained about food after that. They were too focused on the project to be petty. Some that were eating less meat discovered that they felt much better. It was a subject the scientists revisited more than once. It was too heated not to ignore.

That night one of the earth nymphs noticed both Fred and Dave eating and sitting next to each other. She smiled at both of them. She had learned from the other earth nymphs they were brothers. From their and her observations, she knew one of them could make her a good mate. The other would only be good for a good time.

She wanted to settle down with someone. She wanted a child. She attracted the attention of both of the brothers. They didn't noticed much else the rest of the night with her around. After the meal was over, Fred approached her.

"Hello, I'm Fred and you are?"

"Raelina."

Dave followed his brother. "Raelina, that's quite a beautiful name."

She smiled at both of them.

"Oh, I'm Dave. Fred is my brother."

"Yes, I noticed that."

Dave smiled. "How long have you been watching us?"

"I don't know. We noticed when you all started to arrive. No one has lived here in quite some time. I know you're one of the scientists. And Fred is building something he calls a spaceship."

"Yep, she's been watching us." Fred chuckled.

"You talk to your spaceship."

Dave laughed. "That's not surprising."

Fred shook his head. "With a brother like you, I don't need any enemies."

Raelina laughed. "It's good to see that you two get along well. I've seen others who were siblings and it was clear that they absolutely hated each other."

"Well, we've had our moments. Right, Dave?"

"We're over those moments, Fred."

They bumped their fists together. She smiled at them. Other earth nymphs chatted with Dr. Asimov and Hal. Others were chatting off in other small groups. It was just the beginning of an alliance between humans and earth nymphs.

Chapter 5 Romance is in the Solar System

Fred still worked on his spaceship, but he noticed one of the earth nymphs was hanging around his brother. He watched them from a distance. It made him sad even though he could still find plenty of women to spend time with. It was just Raelina. Yet, there was something about her that even Fred couldn't deny.

He wasn't sure if he should feel jealous or happy for his brother. He sighed. He watched them more and realized that he might have to leave her alone. He went to visit Dr. Asimov's house. The older man wasn't home, but Hal was.

"Come in, Fred. Dr. Asimov is busy with the earth nymphs right now. Is there something I can help you with?"

"Yeah, can I look over those diagrams for an android again?"

"Sure. They're right here." Hal handed over the information. "Do you have any questions about androids?"

"Yeah, I do. Dr. Asimov suggested that I build a robot to help me run the ship. I think it's a good idea."

"I noticed you've made a lot of progress with your ship lately. How close are you to completion?"

"I don't know. The four drives are installed. So is the computer. But I need to add some living space to it. I've been having a little trouble with that lately."

"I'm sure you'll come up with something sooner or later."

"Well, perhaps I have an idea. I was looking into having a decent kitchen and living room. A bathroom of course. A medical bay and a couple of bedrooms. In case I have guests."

"That sounds pretty comfortable for a bachelor."

"Yeah, that's what I was thinking. But I may need to robot to help with upkeep. Like cleaning or other things that I may forget to do as far as maintenance goes."

"Dr. Asimov mentioned there would be a lot to do on a spaceship by yourself. But with a robot, it shouldn't be so bad. I'm sure you will be fine if you build one."

"Yeah." Fred studied the diagrams. "I like this design, but where am I going to get all these parts?"

"I'd be happy to help."

"Really? Won't you get in trouble?"

"No. I'm allowed to get my hands on those items."

Fred smiled. "Good. But I don't want a male android. I want a female."

"That can be arranged. If you look here and here, you'll see there is a design for a female."

"Oh, yes. Very good. Can we change the coloring of her hair and skin?"

"Sure. What colors do you want?"

"Green for both. And green eyes."

Hal blinked. Made no comment as to whom Fred could be thinking about. "Let me make those notes." He made the adjustments. "There. How's she look to you?"

"Beautiful."

"Good. She will be highly intelligent. If you don't treat her well, she won't let you get away with it."

Fred laughed. "Good. I like them feisty. It will make the dullness of space travel go by faster."

Hal smiled. He helped Fred to finalized the plans for the new android. Neither told anyone that they were collecting parts and building one. Fred was the one who decided her name would be Starfire. Hal made a note of the name. From then on they just mentioned the name and nothing more.

The earth nymphs knew Fred was up to something a bit more than just the spaceship. But no one questioned him. They found it more fun to watch him building and designing than asking him questions. It was obvious to everyone that Fred enjoyed working on his spaceship. But there were some who were beginning to wonder if it could fly.

Would it work when the time came? There was only one way for Fred to find out. But it wasn't time for that yet.

Fred left the house to return to his spaceship. He had the notes about the android on his tablet computer. He checked the ship's computer and uploaded the notes.

"Hey, you busy?"

Fred turned to see Raelina. "No."

"Good because I wanted to talk to you before you hear it from someone else."

"Hear what?"

"About Dave and me."

"I've noticed."

"Oh. Okay."

He sighed.

"I'm sorry. I don't want to break your heart. I don't want to take your brother from you either."

"But you prefer him to me?"

"Yes."

"Why?"

"He's faithful and he'll settle down."

"Oh. Then you should be with him."

"Fred, don't be sad."

"Raelina, you've made your choice. I am happy for you and Dave."

"But you're sad. You're heart is breaking. I'm so sorry."

"Don't be. Enjoy my brother. He will give you what you prefer better than I ever could."

"Would you break all ties with your brother?"

"No. Did he ask you to marry him?"

"No."

"Oh, I see."

"Okay, I just wanted to make sure you'd be alright with Dave and me."

"I'll be fine. Don't worry."

"Okay." She turned and walked away.

He watched her go. He sighed. He had no idea what he would say to his brother if she was brought up in conversation. Fred set his tablet down. He sat down on the floor. He let his head fall to his lap. He didn't stop the tears from falling. His body shook. He held on to himself. No one saw him. He was hidden by his ship.

It wasn't too long after that when Dave gave him the news. Dave and Raelina had just gotten engaged. They weren't waiting very long. Just a little wedding and they both wanted Fred to be there. Fred agreed to be at their wedding. But his sadness grew for a time.

Chapter 6 Wedding

Once again, Fred had to wear a monkey suit. He was uncomfortable, but it was for his brother and soon to be sister-in-law. Fred forced himself to smile. Soon he found he could smile without faking. He was happy for them. He wasn't the least bit surprised that his brother was the one who was going to settle down.

Fred didn't think he would ever settle down. Not when there were plenty to play with and he didn't have to worry about having to see them again. He did try to avoid those who wanted any form of commitment. It was just a rule he gave himself. It was just fun and nothing serious. So far, he had been a good judge of the difference. The last thing he wanted was to leave a trail of broken hearts behind him.

He had heard of stories in which guys didn't care if the women were hurt afterwards. It didn't end well for the guys. Besides, Fred had a healthy respect for women to know it was better not to push. If they wanted to, they'd come to him. They'd let him know. He never had to chase anyone. All he had to do was let them know he was interested.

He blinked. Soon others had gathered for the wedding. Dr. Asimov and Hal sat down with other scientists and their families. Fred stood by near the arch. He was waiting like everyone else for the bride and groom to show up. No one had to wait long for them.

They walked hand and hand down the aisle. Everyone stood up for them. Dave wore his suit. Raelina wore a fancy dress that looked like she was covered in multicolored leaves. They stopped at the arch and turned to face each other. They held their hands and looked into each other's eyes.

Everyone else, including Fred, sat down. Dave and Raelina exchanged their vows. Some people cried. Others smiled. Dave and Raelina kissed. Fred and others cheered. People applauded the newly wedded couple. Someone turned some music on. Dave and Raelina danced alone.

When the next song came on, others joined in. Fred didn't dance. Neither did Hal. Hal walked over to Fred.

"Fred, the parts are here now."

"Good. When do you have time for us to build Starfire?"

"We could do it as soon as we can leave the wedding."

Fred smiled. "I don't know how long my brother and his wife want to keep dancing."

"Judging by the way they are looking at each other, it doesn't look like it won't be much longer than another hour before they go home."

"I told them I wasn't going to be home tonight. I have already moved into my spaceship."

"That certainly helps."

"Yes, I figured they wanted some privacy, especially for

tonight."

After an hour, Dave and Raelina said goodnight to everyone. They walked hand in hand to their home. No one saw them until the next morning at breakfast. Everyone else dispersed.

Hal and Fred went to Hal's place first to get the parts. They hauled them over to Fred's spaceship. Dr. Asimov watched them, but said nothing. He smiled when they left his house. It didn't take them long to get everything to the spaceship.

Starlover was finished. It had taken quite a bit of time, but the spaceship was ready for testing. It was sparsely furnished. Just the way Fred liked it. But it had what was essential for living and working on board a spaceship. Except for a robot.

Fred had added a secret room and that's where he led Hal to with the parts. He knew how some people could react to androids if they knew. He figured the secret room could be the android's. A place where Starfire could hide when she needed to be hidden from view.

Hal looked around the room. He pulled out the diagrams and soon they worked on putting the parts together. It didn't take them long to get the android together. Hal opened the last box to reveal an outfit which fit the android perfectly.

"Well, how does she look?"

"Beautiful."

She looked very much like Raelina. But neither spoke that out loud.

"We need to turn her on."

"Oh, yes, of course."

Hal turned the new android on. No one said anything. Starfire looked around her. She blinked her eyes. She raised her hands and looked at them. Hal stood in front of her.

"Hello, Starfire. How are you today?"

She blinked and lowered her hands. "Oh, I'm fine. Thanks. How are you?"

"I'm fine."

"Is that you, Hal?"

"Yes."

She looked at the other person in the room. "Are you Fred?"

"Yes." Fred looked to Hal. "Did you program her before we put her together?"

"Yes. She doesn't know very much just yet, but she can learn. I was trying to make it easier for you when we turned her on."

"Oh, I didn't think of that."

"I thought you weren't thinking of that. I thought it would be easier if she already knew language and knew who you are."

"How much did you tell her about me?"

"Just the little that I know."

Fred smiled. "I think that does help. Starfire, do you know where you are?"

"I'm in a room."

"This is your room. It is a part of the spaceship *Starlover*."

"The one you built?"

"Yes."

"Is it finished?"

"Yes."

"Can I have a schematic of the ship?"

"Yes. Over here is a console, where you can access the *Starlover* computer. You can call the computer Starlover."

Starfire activated the console and soon was typing to Starlover. "She knows things I don't."

"That's okay. She has a different function than you do," said Hal.

"Oh. Will you be on this ship with Fred and me?"

"No. I will remain Dr. Asimov's assistant."

"Okay. Just as I will be Fred's assistant."

"Yes," answered Hal.

"It will just be you and me on the ship doing all the work."

"Yes," answered Fred.

"Okay, Fred. I've been programmed to know what all kinds of work a spaceship would need."

"Good. I'm not sure I know everything. I do know how to pilot a ship, so you don't need to worry about that. But I might have trouble talking to Starlover."

"I am programmed to be a translator."

"Wonderful. Sounds like Hal thought of everything. Thanks, Hal."

"It's good to be of service. I believe you can take it from here. I must depart for the evening."

"Goodnight, Hal."

"Goodnight, Fred and good luck."

"Thanks."

Hal let himself off the ship. Fred soon left for his room to change his clothes. Starfire followed him. He took off the monkey suit and put on some more comfortable clothes. She watched him make the changes.

"We might have someone else with us on this test run."

"Oh?"

"Yes, so you should probably stay in your room while he's here."

"I see a mention of that in my starting files. That's why you gave me my own room which is also hidden inside the ship."

"Yes. I figured it would be safer after what Dr. Asimov and Hal said to me about androids."

"Okay. I can stay out of the way whenever there is someone else other than you on board."

"Very good. Well, I need to go out for a drink to talk with the guy to see if he's really interested. I'll be back. Please stay on the ship. You can explore and talk to Starlover while I'm gone."

"Very well. I will do that. Do you know how long you will be gone?"

"I don't know. It shouldn't be too long. Perhaps about an hour or so."

"Okay. See you later, Fred."

"See you later, Starfire."

Chapter 7 Traveling without a Broken Heart?

Fred was back on board his spaceship. He yawned.

"Oh, good you're back."

"Oh, hi. I'm sleepy. I need to go to bed."

"I found my sleeping alcove in my room."

"Good."

"So, is the guy coming?"

"Yeah. I just have tell him how much it costs. I'm too tired right now to think about that part."

"You mean as in he has to pay you some money for coming along with us?"

"Yes. He wants to go to Orcus. I told him I needed to test the ship first. Oh, you can help me with that after I sleep."

"Okay. I can remind you about the fee you want to charge the guy."

"Oh, his name is Dello."

"Dello wants to go to Orcus. Okay, got it. Goodnight, Fred."

"Goodnight, Starfire."

"Have pleasant dreams. I'll do some more exploring quietly so you can sleep."

"Okay."

Fred walked to his quarters. He stripped down to his underwear and crawled into bed. Starfire watched him go to bed and then she resumed her exploration. It didn't take her long to find all the consoles throughout the ship. She and Starlover were starting to communicate wirelessly. It was all just a matter of hardware and learning.

She was fascinated by how Fred had built his ship. She had schematics of other spaceships in her files. She had all the current information on the four different faster than light speed drives installed on the ship. She also knew how to do the repair work if Fred needed help or if he couldn't fix the ship for whatever reason. She also knew Hal's secret. That was part of the reason she knew she had to stay hidden from anyone but Fred. And Hal of course.

She smiled to herself. She and Hal had a special way they could send messages back and forth to each other. In her start up files, he left a secret message that she could contact him if she needed help doing her job. She never told Fred she could contact Hal.

She was exploring the kitchen when Fred walked in. He yawned. He prepared some coffee for himself as she watched him.

"Good morning, Fred."

"Oh, morning," he mumbled. "You're not tired?"

"No, my batteries are still fairly well charged."

"Oh." He got a mug and filled it with coffee. He sat down at the table. "I need to finish this coffee before I'll be ready to do any work today."

"Okay." She sat down next to him. She waited for him to wake up fully. She blinked.

He took his time drinking his coffee. But finish it, he did. "Okay. Do you know how much fuel will cost us?"

"I don't know how much it sells for."

"Oh, that could be a problem. Uh, we'll have to look up the nearest station."

"Will you have to get some fuel to the ship?"

"Probably."

Starlover spoke throughout the ship with a pleasant female voice, "Incoming call for Fred from Hal."

Fred blinked. "Oh? This is early."

"Fred, do you want me to put him on the speakers? He said he doesn't need to see you," Starlover continued.

"Uh, yeah, put him on the speakers."

"Good morning, Fred."

"Good morning, Hal. I wasn't aware that Starlover could take voice commands."

"Oh, she must have learned from Starfire."

"What?"

"Yeah, Starfire and Starlover both have wireless hardware. Sorry, I thought you knew."

"Oh, wow. That certainly makes things easier." Fred paused. "So why are you calling me so early?"

"It's late morning."

Fred chuckled.

"I thought you'd like some fuel for Starlover. I got some this morning. We just need to fill the tank."

"How did you know how much fuel to get?"

"I asked Starlover."

Fred laughed. "And of course she would know how much she needs. Thanks, Hal. You're a genius."

Hal laughed. "Okay, you caught me. I did give Starlover some programming as well. I had a feeling that you'd need some help. I didn't think you ever had a spaceship in your life before."

"You're right. I haven't. I've just been on shuttles. Which, by the way, Dave is keeping."

"Oh?"

"It doesn't matter. I told him it was okay. He's got a wife. I think he'll need it more than I will. I'm leaving the planet soon."

"Yes, you are. So you coming out here so we can give Starlover some fuel?"

"Yeah, give me fifteen minutes. I need a shower and a shave."

"Okay, I can wait."

Starlover spoke again. "Hal has disconnected."

"Thanks, Starlover."

"You're welcome, Fred."

Fred stood up. Put his coffee mug in the sink. He walked to the bathroom. Starfire followed him.

"You may not want to keep following me all over the ship. You can be independent of me."

"Okay." She stood in the hallway as he went into the bathroom by himself.

Soon he had his shower. He came out of the bathroom with a towel wrapped around his waist. He went into his bedroom and found some clean clothes. He put on his shoes and combed his hair. He looked at Starfire.

"I hope you stay on the ship while Hal and I fill up the tank."

"I will. I can watch on one of the screens."

"Okay. That's fine."

Fred left the ship to meet Hal. Starfire found a console and watched them on the screen. She could hear them talking through the spaceship's speakers.

"Ah, there you are." Hal smiled.

"Yeah, I know. I just got up not that long ago."

"Another late night?"

"Oh, not like that. I have a passenger to take. I need to figure out what to charge him and test the ship."

"Sounds like a busy day."

"Yeah, it will be."

Hal set up the hose and connected it to the ship. Soon the fuel was transferred from the temporary tank to the ship.

"So why go to all this trouble?"

"I wanted to help."

"That's nice of you."

"Dr. Asimov knows I've helped you out."

"Yeah, what does he think about that?"

"He said it was fine. I know he's curious about what you're doing and hopes you'll do well."

"Perhaps I should say goodbye to him before I leave."

"He'd like that."

"Okay."

They finished up and Hal left. Fred went back on the ship. Starfire was in a corridor standing in front of a console.

"Alright, now we need to figure out what to charge for passage to Orcus."

He looked at the screen and saw some figures. He looked more closely. "Oh! You were working on that while I was outside. That figure looks reasonable considering how much fuel and food cost. Let me send that to him."

"Starfire?" Fred looked around, but he couldn't see her.

"Yes, Fred," she answered through the speakers.

"Where are you?"

"I'm studying the bathroom."

"Oh. I'm meeting with Dello once more. I'll be out for a while."

"Okay."

"He's already paid me, so that shouldn't be a problem. I'll be back."

"I'll stay on the ship."

Fred smiled and left for his meeting. They met in a bar and it went well. An hour later Fred was walking back to his ship. Once he was back on board, he called, "Starfire?"

"Yes, Fred." She appeared at his side.

"Dello will be here tomorrow morning."

"Okay. As soon as he's near, I'll make sure I'm in my room."

"Good. I think we will travel to Venus first to make sure everything is good with the drives. Then we'll fly to Orcus."

"Okay. Got it."

"Have you finished studying the ship?"

"Yes. You have some interesting and different designs."

"Thank you."

"I've made notes so I know what to do differently than what my original files state."

"I'm used to improvising."

"Noted. Will you take suggestions?"

"I'm always open to suggestions. I still have a lot to learn as you do."

She nodded. "Is it your bedtime again?"

He yawned. "Yes. I'll see you in the morning."

The next morning Fred got up. "Starfire?"

"Yes, Fred," she answered through the speakers.

"I'm going to say goodbye to Dr. Asimov and Hal. I want to do that before Dello arrives."

"I'll let you know when he arrives."

"I'll be watching as well. I shouldn't be that far from the ship."

"Okay. Noted."

Fred took a shower and then got dressed. He left the ship for Dr. Asimov's house. Fred didn't have to knock. Both Dr. Asimov and Hal stepped out and greeted him.

"I hope this isn't the last that we hear of you," said Dr. Asimov.

"No, it doesn't have to be. We can keep in touch."

"Good. I look forward to hearing about your adventures."

"Oh, it looks like my passenger is coming. I need to meet him. Goodbye, Dr. Asimov, Hal. Thanks for all your help."

"Goodbye," both Dr. Asimov and Hal said at the same time.

Fred walked back to his ship to greet Dello.

"Good morning, Dello."

"Good morning, Fred. This is all I have left."

"That's fine. You'll have a whole room to yourself. But we have to share the bathroom."

"Okay. It looks bigger than I thought it would."

"Oh, it has four faster than light speed drives and comfortable living space. There's even a medical bay."

"Wow, you really thought it out."

"I've been building things for years. This was just one more challenge for me to take on."

Dello smiled. "Well, I'm ready for takeoff whenever you say."

"Good." Fred turned when he saw his brother and sister-in-law.

Hand in hand Raelina and Dave approached Fred. They watched him standing with someone next to his spaceship. Raelina smiled.

"Fred, it's beautiful. Does it have a name?"

"Yes, her name is Starlover."

"That's a good name," she said.

"Bro, you know you're welcome to visit us."

"Yes, I know. But now I want to see the solar system."

"Oh, who's with you?" she asked.

"This is Dello. My brother Dave and his wife Raelina. Dello is my passenger."

"Oh, wow. So you'll be earning some money with this spaceship?" Dave smiled.

"Yeah. We're going to head to Orcus for a bit. I don't know where after that."

"Well, goodbye and keep in touch, Fred." Raelina hugged him.

He hugged her back. Dave and Fred hugged. Fred watched his brother and sister-in-law walk away. He turned to Dello and they boarded *Starlover*. After Dello set his bag down in his room, they went to the bridge. Fred raised the ship and soon they were in outer space. It was quite a sight for both of them.

Fred decided to fly towards Venus. Starlover was doing well.

"Just as beautiful as your reputation claims, Lady Venus. I'll be back to spend some time with you." Fred smiled. "Okay, now it's time for Orcus."

"Sounds good to me. I may end up staying there."

"Okay, if that's what you want."

Fred plotted the new flight path with Starlover and Starfire.

Chapter 8 Settling In

"Dave, have you met our next door neighbors? They are the Lutins."

"They are? You mean Jean Lutin?"

"Yes, and her husband George."

"Oh, I've met Jean. She's one of the scientists on this project."

Raelina laughed. "So, you've at least met her."

"Well, yeah, we work together."

"I know. But what about her husband?"

"Oh, that must be who she sits next to at meals. I wondered if there was something going on with all that flirting they tend to do."

Raelina laughed again.

"You think we should socialize with them?"

"Yes."

"Um, okay. You're better at it than I am. So is my brother."

"Really?"

"Yeah. When Fred and I were leaving our parents' house, he suggested we go to the bar to pick up women. We did go and flirt with some women, but we didn't pick any up. He was definitely better at flirting and socializing with them than I was."

She smiled. "I'll be with you. Don't you worry."

"Okay."

"We can talk to them at the evening meal, when you're more

likely ready to relax."

"Okay."

"Until then, I wanted to show and ask you something."

"What?" He followed her.

"That! I thought you humans used water ones. That doesn't require water."

He chuckled. "That's part of the project. Using water for our wastes is wasteful. We don't need to create blackwater. Grey water is okay because as long as we don't use anything toxic, we can use it to water plants."

"Oh!"

"Yeah, and we have to mix some sawdust into it to help keep the smell down and to help it decompose."

"Okay."

"We just have to be careful where we dump our wastes to prevent the spread of disease."

"You have that problem?"

"Unfortunately, we have documented cases of it happening."

"I see." She walked to the kitchen. "So, why have this room at all, if we all eat together at regular mealtimes?"

"Good questions. I think it's a habit to have some sort of kitchen. We don't have an oven in here. Just one induction burner." He paused to look around the kitchen. "I suppose we do have them so people can have coffee or tea first thing in the morning. Or at any time of the day."

"Well, it's nice to be able to get a glass of water whenever I need it. I don't have to go very far. Just to the sink."

"There is always that. At least the water is purified and we have the option of adding minerals to it."

"You have been thinking of lots of little things."

"It's the little things which add up. If we don't pay attention, they can cause huge problems."

"Like eating too much in the way of animal and animal products?"

"Yes. We've come close to losing some plants because of that. Vanilla and chocolate are now very expensive. We almost lost coffee for the same reason."

"I see. No wonder my people are upset with humans in general."

"Can't say I blame them."

"Yet, there have always been some, like you, who care enough to do something about it."

"Did your people appear to those humans?"

"Oh, yes, they did. We've always been peaceful. We stayed away from those who would destroy the planet for the sake of money and not care about the consequences to themselves or others."

"I don't blame you. They can be hard to get through to."

"My people have stories about trying to stop those humans without success. The earth nymphs were always killed as a result."

He grimaced. "I can see why you wouldn't want to deal with those humans." He looked at her. "Do you have any other questions about our house?"

"No, not really."

"It's not as high tech as many houses are these days, but we don't really need that much to prove our point."

"Actually, the high tech would just baffle me. That tablet of yours is enough tech for me to deal with."

"You never use it."

"I don't need it."

"Hmm. I never thought about it. I'm used to using some kind of computer."

"We've never needed any tech to live our lives."

"Perhaps you wouldn't. You can live right in nature so much easier than us humans can."

"This is true. We love it that we can."

"But yet you married me and you're living with me in this house."

She nodded. "But sometimes I have to go into the ground or else I could die."

"Oh, okay."

"You're remembering when we first came here."

"Yes. We thought the greenery was acting funny. There was no wind and then you and your people showed up. Formed into humanoid right in front of us."

"We thought you could handle it. We've watched you for quite a long time."

"How long?"

"Since you first came here."

"When we started the project?"

"Dr. Asimov and Hal were the first ones here."

"Yes."

"Then you and your brother came next."

"Yes. Then everyone else started to come after that."

"We didn't know why any humans would want to come back here when no one's lived here for at least a century. So, of course we were curious. When we learned why you came, we wanted to work with you. It was our chance to restore the balance back to a healthy planet."

"We do like this partnership."

"I know."

"But with us, it's also very personal."

"And good."

She approached him. Put her arms around his neck. She leaned closer to him and kissed him. It didn't take long for it to become deeper and more passionate. He picked her up and carried her to their bedroom.

At the evening meal, Raelina took Dave by the hand and had

them sit next to the Lutins. Everyone smiled at each other.

"Hi, Raelina," said Jean.

"Hi, Jean and George," answered Raelina.

"Hi, Jean, I didn't realize you were married," said Dave.

Jean laughed. "Well, I suppose it's because I'm so independent people tend to overlook him."

George smiled. "I'm a writer. I'm documenting the project so that others can read about our adventures and misadventures as they may be."

Raelina turned to Dave. "He's been blogging about us. Just about the project and what we've done so far."

"Yes, I have. I hope that's not a problem."

Dave shook his head. "No, I know I requested a writer to help document Project Earth, but I didn't realize it was you. I guess I'm too focused on my part to have noticed the whole picture."

George shook Dave's hand. "No worries. My wife got in because she's a hard core scientist. I'm just a writer. But after we get far enough along, I will compile the blog posts into a book. The royalties will go to support environmentally sound non-profit organizations."

"Wonderful. I'm glad you're here. I wouldn't be able to blog with everything I have going on with this project."

"And you just got married not that long ago. That's a real adjustment." George laughed. "But it's worth it. I wouldn't have it any other way."

"We're pretty happy together as well."

The couples continued to talk throughout the meal. Dave was glad Raelina had suggested it.

Chapter 9 Children

"Dave?"

"Yes, Raelina?"

"I feel funny."

"Funny how?"

"Well, I'm hungry all the time. Eating doesn't seem to relieve it. I have lots of varied food cravings. And now I can feel something moving in my belly."

Dave stopped cold. "Uh…"

"Will I be alright?"

"I hope so."

"What's wrong with me?"

"Uh, let's go see the doctor. She'll know what it is."

They walked to the medical house hand in hand. They walked inside. The doctor was reading something on her tablet computer. She looked up when they walked in.

"What's happened?" the doctor asked.

"Uh, she feels funny. From what she described, it sounds like she could be pregnant."

The doctor smiled. "Let me scan her." She picked up her portable scanner and ran it above Raelina's belly. "Oh, yes, it's a baby. And you're both doing well."

"Oh, is that why I'm so hungry?"

"Yes, and eat as much as you want. The baby needs it just as much as you do."

"Okay."

"Do you have any morning sickness?"

"What's that?"

"Do you ever feel nauseous?"

"No. Just hungry."

"Consider yourself lucky. I don't see any sign of nutritional deficiencies. So, I'd say you should be fine."

"Good. I'm glad it's no big deal."

"How are you taking it, Dave?"

"Uh…"

The doctor laughed. "She's fine. Just let her eat. I think what we have here is fine. Doesn't seem to be causing her any trouble."

He nodded. "Right. Okay, come on, let's find you some food."

"Okay. See you, Doctor!"

The doctor waved goodbye and resumed her reading.

Raelina and Dave went to the community garden. They watered. They weeded. They found some food that was ripe. They harvested it. They took it back to their house. She chopped it up and made a salad. He checked his tablet to see what else he needed to get done. He sat at the kitchen table. She joined him with her big salad and a glass of water.

By the time he was done checking his notes and research materials, she was done eating the salad. They looked at each other.

"Did that help with the hunger?"

"For now. But I may get hungry again in a couple of hours." She took the dirty dishes to the sink. She washed them.

"By then it will be time for the evening meal."

"Good."

At the evening meal, Raelina and Dave sat down next to Jean and George. Jean noticed Raelina taking seconds.

"Expecting, Raelina?"

Raelina blinked and looked at Jean. "What does that mean?"

"Are you pregnant, dear? I've not seen you eat so much."

"Yes."

"Oh, I am too." Jean helped herself to seconds. "It's good to know I'm not the only one."

"I'm hungry a lot now."

"So am I. Anything else?"

"No, nothing bad. The doctor says I should be fine."

"She told me the same thing. I feel pretty good even though someone is growing inside of me."

"How long will the baby grow before they come out?"

"Oh, about nine months."

"Oh, that seems like a long time."

"The baby will be born soon enough. You'll see. You'll get to the point where you may want the baby to come out."

"You mean the baby will just get so big and we have to keep carrying them around?"

"Yes. Lots of women complain of back problems when carrying a baby, especially in the latter days of pregnancy."

"Oh, I don't think I'll like that part."

"Neither do I, but we'll find a way to endure it."

"Yes, because they are our babies."

Months later Raelina and Jean found themselves in labor. Both had their husbands helping them get to the medical house. Neither really had any trouble with the labor, other than being exhausted afterwards. The babies were strong and healthy. Raelina and Dave had a girl they named Lizette Cassandra. Jean and George had a boy they named Jaekob.

Raelina had no trouble caring for her daughter when still just a baby. Jean made sure she got a sling so she could carry her baby around while she was working. She didn't think having a baby to care for exempted her from the work she was doing on the project.

Chapter 10 Notes from the Kuiper Belt

As they were nearing Orcus, Starlover gave them a few different angles to view the planet. They were a long way from the sun. Dello was sitting next to Fred. Dello watched the screens and did nothing else. Fred watched the screen and checked the instruments. It was his first spaceship landing. But not the first landing he had ever done. He had landed shuttles plenty of times. This was just a larger vehicle. It required more space.

But they had that on Orcus. Fred landed the ship safely. He and Dello walked to the airlock. Through the window they could see two people extending a tunnel from the biodome to the spaceship. Once the tunnel was connected, Fred opened the airlock. The two people walked back a little ways down the tunnel to stand with the rest of the welcoming committee.

Della smiled. "Welcome to Orcus, boys."

Fred smiled. "It's a pleasure to meet you, ladies." He bowed and saw Teo. "Oh! and good to see you too, kind sir."

Teo chuckled.

Dello smiled. "Hello, everyone."

They all walked back to the square with Della leading the way. Once they got there, Lila set Kim down. Kim ran around and danced. The adults laughed. Della soon introduced everyone. Fred saw Dello say something privately to Della.

Soon everyone was chatting and getting to know the first visitors. Their reputations were scrutinized, but appreciated by the twins and Della. The others just shook their heads. The twins didn't waste time making plans with Fred. Dello didn't want to join. He said he had already made plans. The twins took Fred by the hand and led him away from the square.

They took him inside their personal house. He saw the huge bed in the center of the room. He smiled. It was the first time he had enjoyed a pair of twins.

"Dello!"

"Hi, Fred."

"So, you sticking around?"

"Yes. You can go. Thanks for the lift. I just need to get my stuff."

"Sure, no problem. It was great having you aboard."

"I enjoyed my trip. You're a good host."

"But I bet Della was even better."

Dello laughed. "Well, there's no competition there."

They boarded the ship. Dello grabbed his already packed bag.

"You staying long?"

"No, I think I want to go exploring the solar system now."

"You should say goodbye to everyone."

"Alright, I'll do that. Let's go."

They left the ship and walked back to the main square of the capital. The amazons were standing around. Even the children were out playing together. Della smiled at both Dello and Fred.

"Are you staying or leaving, boys?" asked Della.

"I'm staying, if you don't mind," said Dello.

"Good. I want you to stay. Fred?"

"I'll be taking my leave of you all. It's been fun. I'm impressed by the work you've done to build this colony."

"Thank you. We all worked hard."

"Joeni and Jaena, that was great. We might have to have a repeat if we see each other again."

The twins smiled and blew him kisses as they waved goodbye. Fred bowed to everyone present and said goodbye. He turned and walked through the tunnel to his ship. He closed the airlock. He waited for two people to detach the tunnel and take it back to their biodome. He waved to them. Turned and went to the bridge.

"Time for takeoff, ladies."

"Acknowledged," both Starfire and Starlover said at the same time.

"Where to, Fred?"

"Oh, I don't know. Let's just fly around the Kuiper Belt. I'm sure we can handle being in space for quite some time."

Starlover said, "Of course we can. I also turn on the artificial gravity just for you so you don't have to float everywhere."

"I never thought about that…"

"There are a lot of things you don't think about. But you're still new to this. You have me and Starfire to help you out."

"Yes, I do." He strapped himself in. "Are we ready for take-off?"

"Yes." Starlover counted down.

The ship lifted up in the sky. Soon a field of black full of stars filled the viewscreen. Fred smiled. He had looked forward to sights like these for quite some time. He didn't engage any of the faster than light speed drives. He just wanted to fly for a bit and look at the stars. He saw Orcus get smaller. It seemed to take forever for it to completely disappear.

He spent hours just sitting in the pilot's seat flying aimlessly. He knew Starlover and Starfire would take over if they thought there was any danger. But for now, he could just fly the ship wherever and be fine. The view was spectacular. He kept at it for hours. Until he was hungry. Then he let Starlover take over the controls so he could go eat in his kitchen.

Chapter 11 Danger Approaches Project Earth

It seemed such an ordinary day. Everyone was going about their business without much worry. Hal watched them as he usually did. But he sensed there were more people around. Certainly a few children had been born in their group. But these seemed like different people. Hal made some internal notes.

He knew quickly the newcomers weren't human or earth nymphs. He wasn't sure what they were at first. He kept his observations to himself. For now it seemed like enough. But something nagged him. He found Dr. Asimov studying something. The old man was so absorbed that he didn't notice the younger man approach him. A shadow fell over Dr. Asimov. He jumped and looked up.

"Oh, it's you, Hal."

"I'm sorry. Was I too quiet for you?"

"Yes, but no matter."

"I'm not sure what to do except for making notes and just observing."

"What's wrong?"

"There are more people nearby. They're not human or earth nymphs. I'm not sure what they are. But they are watching us."

"Oh?"

"Well, do you have any idea who they could be?"

"No. Are you aware of Herbert Mineur's controversial notes

from his time on Mars?"

"No, but I am aware he was one of the first colonists on Mars."

"Read his notes. He talks about water nymphs, were creatures, and vampires. All people we previously thought were fictional."

"Right, but we now know earth nymphs are real. Some of them are helping with Project Earth now."

"Yes, but the general public may not have accepted them."

"I'll keep that in mind." Hal consulted a tablet computer. "I see his notes are readily available."

"Yes, but many people don't accept them even though he was quite thorough and provided quite a bit of biological evidence."

"He was a biologist and a skeptic. He would have demanded biological evidence or else he wouldn't have written this. Correct?"

"That is correct. He wouldn't even have been chosen for the mission if he wasn't that good of a scientist."

"I only know him by reputation."

"So do I."

Hal sat down and read Herbert Mineur's notes. He made mental notes on the different type of humanoids the biologists had discovered. The evidence was compelling. Hal could see why many wouldn't accept it even with the biological evidence. He set the tablet down. Dr. Asimov looked at him.

"Well, did you find your answer as to who's watching us now?"

"No. I don't have enough evidence about them."

"Just keep observing them."

"I will. I know I'm the only one who can."

"You are unique, unless that Fred built something you don't want to talk about."

"You know I couldn't tell even if he did."

Dr. Asimov smiled. "I know. We've kept your secret well."

Hal smiled. "Hopefully, no one will find out."

"Well, I won't tell and I could die any minute now."

"I know, but you're still here. Why is that?"

"I don't know. I would have thought my body would have worn out by now."

"Unless you're really an android in disguise."

Dr. Asimov laughed.

Fred was in the pilot's seat once again. "I think it's time to plot a course to Venus. I want to go to the floating city of Aphrodite. I hear it will be a great time for me."

Starlover said, "Plotting a course to Venus. The course is set. Select a drive and we can fly there."

Fred smiled. He selected a drive and soon they were headed to Venus. He watched Neptune get closer. Then it was gone. Next was Uranus. Jupiter stayed the longest on the viewscreen. Then it was the asteroid field. Then Mars. Earth. Finally Venus came into view. He was excited.

He contacted the local air traffic control to see what he needed to do next.

"Attention, *Starlover*. You may land on our floating airfield. Your ship should fit. How long will you be staying on Venus?"

"How long can I stay?"

"That depends upon your business here."

"Just pleasure."

"Well, in that case, you can leave your ship here for a month. We may have to ask you to leave earlier than that if any large ships need to land."

"Okay. Sounds good to me."

"Very well. We have shuttles for hire that will leave here and come back. We're sending the information on them right now. We're also sending your computer information on how to land on the floating platform."

"Okay. Thank you."

Fred waited for all of the information. He was still at the controls, but Starlover had the coordinates. He would have to let her land the ship this time. He didn't mind. By this time he, Starlover, and Starfire had become a team. He felt comfortable and knew he could trust them with anything.

Starlover brought them into the clouds of Venus. The clouds were yellow and there wasn't much to see at first. But soon he could see the floating platform which was the air strip. It became larger the closer they got. Just before they landed, he could see other ships on top of the platform.

Starlover slowed the ship down considerably before she landed it on the platform. Fred read the message on his screen. "Enjoy your stay here on Venus. A shuttle is standing by when you're ready to visit the cities." He smiled.

"Alright, I trust you ladies will be okay without me for several hours."

"Yes," answered both Starlover and Starfire at the same time.

"Good. I'm going to have some fun. I have a watch on me so I can contact you and you can contact me if anything goes wrong. And of course I can contact a shuttle to bring me back here."

"So noted. Have fun, Fred. See you later."

"Yes, I'll see you two later."

He unstrapped himself and stood up. He walked off the ship and found the shuttle.

"Where would you like to go?"

"Aphrodite."

"Ah, yes, of course."

"Is there any place you'd recommend for a good time?"

"Depends upon what kind of fun you're looking for." Fred smiled.

"If you're just wanting to look, there are plenty of dancers in the clubs. But if you want to touch, then you need to look for the red lights just above the doors."

"Sounds good to me. What else is there?"

"There's casinos if you feel like losing your money to us." The pilot chuckled as he took off of the platform.

"I'll probably be too busy with the ladies."

"Suit yourself."

Chapter 12 Starlover, Starfire, & Fred

"What is it, Fred?" asked Starfire.

"I don't know. I have an idea to get a computer chip imbedded in my brain so I can communicate faster and easier with you and Starlover, especially when someone else is around."

"Would that be safe for you?"

"I think it's possible. But I don't know what kind of chip."

"I can design one for you."

"You can?"

"Yes. I can also install it in your brain."

"Whoa. Then let's get started on the design."

They went to the repair station. They consulted Starlover for a proper chip and design. It took some time, but eventually, the chip was ready. It would give Fred the ability to talk to both Starlover and Starfire without speaking out loud. He would become the biological counterpart to them.

"Are you ready for me to install this chip?"

"Yeah. Let's go to the medical bay."

"Of course."

It didn't take them long to reach the medical bay. He laid down on the bed. She looked down on him. She turned on the bed's scanning equipment.

"I need to give you an anesthetic. So, it's time for you to sleep." She gave him the shot before he could protest.

He closed his eyes and remembered nothing more until he woke up an hour later. The android was standing by watching him.

"How do you feel, Fred?"

"Groggy."

"You should be fine in a few minutes."

"I hope so." He sat up. "What am I doing here?"

"You asked for a chip to be planted into your brain so you can communicate with me and Starlover without talking out loud."

"Oh, I do remember thinking that's what I wanted. But we designed it?"

"Yes. Starlover and I gave our input and helped you create one you can use. Why don't you try it?"

"Oh." He closed his mouth and thought, "Starlover, can you hear me?"

"Yes," he could hear inside his head and not through the speakers.

He tried again. "Starfire, can you hear me?"

"Yes, Fred." Again he heard the answer inside his head. "Wow!" he said out loud. "Will this work when I'm off the ship?"

Inside his head he heard both Starlover and Starfire. "Of course. It's similar to our hardware which allows us to communicate wirelessly."

"Okay," he answered in his head. He paused. He went on with the silent communication. "I have a date." He checked his watch. "Oh, I better get going." He requested a shuttle.

He left the ship a few minutes later. The shuttle was there and soon he was off to Aphrodite. He was looking forward to this date even though he was essentially paying her for services. He didn't care. She had seemed sad when they had met. But she was working. Fred respected that. He had heard from some other guys that she was good.

So he had approached her and set up a time to have some fun. He was almost late. But he was able to walk quickly to the place. He had just barely made it on time. He checked in at the front desk. She came down within a few minutes.

"Hello, Fred. I'm Viki. This way to my room."

He followed her. In his head he heard Starfire talking. "Oh, what are you going to do with her?"

"It's just a little bit of fun. Will you leave me alone for a little while?" he answered back silently.

"Okay." Starfire was silent.

He smiled. She ushered him into her private room. He saw the massage table and the oils. He also saw the large bathtub and a large bed. He nodded. "This looks good."

"Would you like to start with the massage?"

"Yes."

"You can step behind the screen and change into a robe."

He stepped behind the designated screen. He took off his clothes and slipped on the robe. He came out and laid down on the massage table. She started and kneaded his muscles. She used oils. He decided she was as good as they said.

"Did I already pay for the works from you?"

"Yes. And thank you."

"No need to thank me. You're doing a great job already."

"But you are helping my daughter."

"You have a daughter?"

"Yes, it was an accident. By the time I realized I was pregnant, he was gone to who knows where those military guys go."

"Would he care to see his own daughter?"

"No, it's better that he doesn't know."

Fred heard the catch in her voice. He said nothing out of politeness.

"I had to send her to an orphanage."

"How old is she?"

"Four years old."

"I have a niece who's five."

"Oh? Have you seen her?"

"Yeah, via a screen. She was born after I built my spaceship. I've been traveling around the solar system for quite some time now."

"How many people on your ship?"

"Just me."

"You must get lonely."
"That's why I called you."
She chuckled. "That's what many of my clients say."
"Well, you are as good as they say."
"I've just started."
"Oh, you mean it could get better from here on out?"
"I'll do my best."
He smiled.

Chapter 13 S.O.S.

Raelina ran as fast as she could. She found a computer console. Soon she was attempting to contact Fred. He was her only hope.

"Come on, answer me, Fred!"

She waited. Her eyes darted around the room. There was nowhere to hide. They would find her sooner or later.

Starlover answered the call. "I'm sorry, Fred is out at the moment, but I can take a message."

"What? Tell him it's important. This is Raelina, his sister-in-law. Project Earth is under attack! We don't know who they are or what they want. They refuse to talk to us. But people are getting attacked. Sometimes all we find is their dead bodies. We can't defend ourselves. Fred, come save us! Your niece needs you. Please. Help us!"

She cried and the connection was cut by someone else who was hiding near her. Starlover had recorded the message. Soon Starfire saw it and wondered who Raelina was. She looked too familiar to Starfire. The android found a mirror and wondered why she looked a lot like Raelina, Fred's sister-in-law. But the android had to wait for Fred to return from his date to ask him.

"Starlover, are we too faraway to try to get a hold of Hal?"

"No. Humans have created network access throughout the

solar system for everyone."

"Good. Hal? Can you hear me?"

"Starfire? This isn't a good time. We're under attack."

"Starlover just got a distress call from Raelina. Starlover recorded it, but the call was cut from her end. What is happening?"

"Some people are attacking us. I don't know who they are. I just keep finding dead bodies. Dr. Asimov is dead."

Starfire gasped. "He created you!"

"Yes, he's dead."

"How many are still alive?"

"I don't know. I don't understand why they aren't attacking me. I'm trying to save the humans and earth nymphs here, but the attackers are too quick for me. I can't see them until it's too late and they've already gone."

"I'm made to look like an earth nymph."

"Yes."

"I look like Raelina. Fred's sister-in-law."

"Yes."

"Oh, no. And Fred is busy on a date. He doesn't want us to bother him."

"Oh… He'll come here if he knows, but I don't know that he can do any good. I feel so useless."

"Hal, hang on. We'll come as soon as we can."

"Okay. I can't stand the screaming. They're so terrified. I just wish I knew who the attackers are and what to do about them."

"Hang on, Hal. This is an emergency. We can keep this line open. Starlover, contact Fred! This is a red alert!"

Sirens blared on the ship.

Starlover spoke softly to Fred. "Fred, we have an emergency. We need you back on the ship."

"What?" asked Fred. "I'm busy on my date. Can't it wait?"

"The people of Project Earth are under attack. They're dying!"

"Oh, shit." He thought about Viki. "Alright, I'll order the shuttle now. But I don't know how long it will be before I reach the ship."

"Acknowledged. We won't leave without you."

"Good."

"Starfire, Fred will be here as soon as he can."

"Did you get that, Hal?"

"Just hurry. I'll see what I can do for the survivors." He sighed mentally.

"Starlover? Can we do anything right now?"

"Just wait for Fred to show up."

Starfire walked around the bridge. "How do humans stand waiting?"

"I've been checking their social media and the answer is: they don't."

"Oh!"

"They deal with waiting in different ways. Many are just so impatient that they yell at other humans."

"Oh, dear."

Fred was enjoying himself. Then he got a message from Starlover. He blinked. He knew Viki wouldn't have heard anything. He tried to pretend for her that he wasn't having that little exchange with his spaceship's computer. Viki had finished what she had promised him. They laid on the bed. He used his watch to contact a shuttle for immediate departure.

It would be another 15 minutes. "Damn."

"What's wrong? Did I do something?"

"No. I just have to get back to my ship as soon as possible."

"Oh?"

"I'm sorry. It's nothing you've done. You were wonderful." He kissed her forehead. "I'd like to come back."

"Really?"

"Yeah." He stood up and grabbed his clothes. He got dressed.

She slipped into a robe. He looked at her. He could see her sadness.

"Do you ever get to see your daughter?"

"Yes. I have an arrangement with the orphanage. I send money for her care. They let me visit her once a week."

"Does she know who you are?"

"I haven't told her. I don't want to. I don't want her to have to do what I do for a living."

"Oh. I hear that."

"I just hope she gets a chance to do something better with her life."

"So do I." His watched beeped. "My ride is here. I'll contact you when I'm back on Venus."

"Okay."

Fred kissed her one more time. This time on her lips with all the passion he felt for her. He smiled and let go of her. He turned and walked out. Within five minutes he was on the shuttle. He tried to keep himself from saying anything to the pilot. He knew it would come out badly if he said anything at all.

He thought to Starlover and Starfire, "I'm on the shuttle. I'll be on board soon, ladies."

"Acknowledged," both answered him inside his head.

Chapter 14 Fred Returns to Earth

"Starfire, prepare for departure."

"Preparing flight pattern," answered Starfire. She sat down and strapped herself into the co-pilot's seat.

Fred sat down and strapped himself into the pilot's seat.

"Which drive?" asked Starlover.

"Adams Improbability."

"Sorry, that drive is offline."

"What?"

"Pick another drive."

"Okay. The Heinlein Irrelevancy Drive."

"Working. Prepare for takeoff."

"*Starlover*, you are clear to leave the airfield."

"Thank you," said Fred.

"The Heinlein Irrelevancy Drive is now offline."

"Oh, come on!"

"The drives need to be repaired."

"We don't have time."

"We still have two left."

"Okay, warp drive."

Starlover lifted the ship off the airfield. It took some time, but soon they were free of Venus' gravitational pull.

"Warp drive is now offline."

"Then give me hyperdrive!"

"Initiating."

Starfire frowned. She saw the readings. She facepalmed herself.

"Hyperdrive is now offline," said Starlover as calm as ever.

"Damn! Then give us whatever we have. What's wrong with the drives?"

"Checking." Starlover displayed on screen what was wrong.

"Oh, shit. We need parts."

"Are we going to make it in time?"

"How should I know? I just hope my brother and everyone else can fight. Someone please be alive when we get there. Don't let Project Earth die like this!" He shook his fist towards the ceiling.

Starfire reviewed the data. "Fred, I think we can repair the Adams' Improbability Drive. We have those parts on hand."

"We do?"

"Yes."

"Then we should just fix it. Otherwise it will take us three months to get to Earth."

They unstrapped themselves and went to the repair station to get tools and the parts they needed. It was the first time they had to repair one of the drives. Fred had made easy access points in case anything were to ever go wrong. He knew when he was building his spaceship that things could and would go wrong no matter if the parts were scrap or brand new.

He and Starfire didn't have much trouble reaching the drive and replacing the parts. When they were done, he was closing up the access point.

Starlover said, "The Adams Improbability Drive is now back online."

"Engage! We've got to get to Earth now!"

"Turning on drive now."

There was a little bit of jolt. Fred fell with his back against one of the walls. Starfire fell into him with her back to him. He put his arms around her waist.

"Fred, are you alright?" asked Starfire.

"Yeah, I'm fine. It's not everyday a beautiful woman falls into me."

The android raised an eyebrow and turned her head to try to see him better. "Are you flirting with me?"

"Oh, I hope that's okay."

She smiled. "I have notes that you really like women from Hal."

He tried to look innocent. "I try to make sure I have permission. I don't force any woman to do anything with me."

"That's good. I have notes of some bad ways that women can be treated."

"Hal gave you that information?"

"He thinks I should know in case I meet anyone who mistakes me for an earth nymph woman."

"Good. You do need to know those things."

"Hal also noted that I should be able to tell you when you cross a line with me that I don't want you to."

"Yeah, do tell me."

"I will."

He let go of her. They went back to the bridge for the remainder of the journey. The spaceship was fine the rest of the trip.

But Fred was another story. He worried about his brother. His sister-in-law. His niece. Dr. Asimov. Hal. Fred closed his eyes. He hoped they could defend themselves from the mysterious attackers. But Raelina looked absolutely terrified when she was contacting him. Then there was the fact that someone, a shadowy figure, had cut the call.

"Fred?"

"Yes, Starfire?"

"What are you thinking?"

They went into their silent communication.

"I'm worried about my family. Who cut the connection on her end? It was probably one of the mysterious attackers."

"You must be fond of her. Or else I wouldn't look like her."

"What? Oh…" He mentally sighed. "But she wanted someone monogamous. My brother is better for her."

"You just accepted that?"

"Yeah. There's no reason to argue with her on that. I couldn't stand to break her heart."

"So you must truly love her. Do you love all the women you play with?"

"Yeah, but it's not the same."

"Oh."

"I don't understand it myself. I don't think I could explain it to you."

"I'm not sure there are other humans who understand such things."

"Have you been researching us?"

"Yes, Starlover and I are studying your social media and whatever else we can get our cyber hands on. You're quite a varied lot."

Fred laughed out loud.

Chapter 15 Monsters!

Raelina screamed. There was nowhere left to run. Dave and a few others were lying dead on the ground. She had no idea where her daughter was. The monsters were moving too fast for her and the other survivors to see where they were from second to second.

Hal ran towards her. He grabbed her without any warning and ran off with her. Soon he found the two of them a safe hiding space.

"Hal?"

"Yes, Raelina?"

"We've got to find Lizette."

"I know. I haven't seen her."

"What about Dr. Asimov?"

"Dead." He paused. "What about Dave?"

"Dead." She cried.

He sighed. He used his tablet computer to scan for the others. "It looks like both Lizette and Jaekob are still alive."

"Where are they?" She looked at the tablet screen.

"I'm not sure about his parents."

"The poor kids."

"It looks like they're hiding together."

"That sounds like a good idea. Who are our attackers?"

"I don't know. I'd say they are monsters. They've attacked

some of your people as well."

"I know. I saw their bodies."

They said no more. Both were thinking of how to get to the children safely and get them all out of the area. But the attackers had other ideas. Hal could still sense one of the monsters a bit too close to him and Raelina. Once again he didn't give her any warning. He put his tablet away.

He grabbed her and ran off with her. This time she didn't protest. She knew Hal had her and would carry her to safety. But she bit her lip thinking about the two five years olds by themselves with the monsters coming after them.

She had no idea how long they had been running. Then suddenly, the monsters jumped in front of them. Hal and Raelina stopped running. They turned to see more pale monsters jumping in front of them. It didn't take long before they were surrounded.

The pale monsters bared their fangs. Raelina screamed. Hal gasped. The pale monsters attacked. Raelina laid on the ground not moving. Hal was still standing fighting off the last of the pale monsters. Then just as quick as they had come, the pale monsters disappeared and left Hal standing by himself.

His clothing was torn and his hair was a mess. He saw Raelina on the ground. He got down beside her to check for a pulse. He scanned her. His mouth gaped open. He had failed to save her.

Jaekob and Lizette were shivering. They tried to be quiet and not cry. The monsters would find them just like they had found the adults. Neither weren't sure if their parents were still alive. All the two kids knew was that they had each other. They had to avoid the monsters as best as they could.

Fortunately, the two five years olds were small. They could crawl and hide into places where the monsters couldn't follow them. But the kids had already been attacked. They were wounded, but they had not seemed to notice. The kids had of course seen some of the dead bodies. The adults they had known their whole lives.

Now the two five years olds were by themselves. They were on their own. They had no idea of the time. Only that they were getting hungry. They had no idea of where to find food. Besides the monsters were still out there. The kids didn't talk. They just stayed together in their hidden place.

Not too far away the kids could still hear the adults screaming. The kids stayed where they were. They didn't even know if they would be rescued or even found where they were. They huddled together and shook terribly. There was nothing more they could do.

Silence prevailed after a time. The kids were exhausted. Still scared and alone. Eventually, they fell asleep by themselves. They were completely unaware about what was going on in the world outside of their hiding place.

Chapter 16 Survivors

"Hal? Are you still alive?"

"Starfire?"

"Oh, good you can hear me. Starlover, Fred, and I are here near Earth now. Are you safe?"

"Yes. The attackers are gone now. But I'm trying to find the children. They are the only ones alive and terribly frightened. I know they're hiding somewhere nearby."

"Okay, Starlover and I can see where they are hiding. They need water, food, and medical attention immediately."

"Oh, I see where they are now."

"Hal, listen to me. This is important. You can't rescue the children. But Fred can. He can't see you. If he does, he won't understand why you're still alive and all the other adults are dead. I'm sure he will give you a medical exam and then he will know your secret."

"Damn. Are you sure the children will be alright until Fred gets to them?"

"Yes. They aren't going to die. Starlover and I don't see any-one else in the area. He's about to land the ship now."

"Alright. Then I'll stay hidden. I'll leave when I know Fred has the children."

"Alright. Do you know who the children are?"

"Yeah, they are the two who were born here. Fred's niece

Lizette and Jaekob Lutin."

"Noted. Should I tell Fred?"

"No. He'll know his niece as soon as he sees her. I don't know if he knows the boy."

"Noted."

Fred landed his spaceship where he had built it. He sighed. He unstrapped himself and stood up.

"Standing by," said Starfire.

"Okay." He looked at the screen in front of him.

Starlover spoke next. "Scanning the area for survivors. There are two, but they are injured. They need medical attention, water, and food."

"Where?"

"Oh, they are small humans. Just children. They appear to be hiding."

"Where?"

A map appeared on the viewscreen. Fred made some mental notes. Then he left his ship. He looked around at the ruins. He gasped to see so many dead just lying on the ground. It was clear that many had been dead for days. He saw both his brother and sister-in-law among the dead. He also found Dr. Asimov.

He sighed and resumed his search for the children. There was debris in the way. He pushed and pulled things out of the way. According to the map he was given, the children should be in a small spot. How was he going to get them out? He sighed and moved more debris.

After an hour, he saw the two children lying in the tight space together. He nearly gasped. They were so dirty. He studied them as closely as he could. He sighed when he saw they were breathing. Perhaps they were just asleep?

"Hey, wake up!" He shouted.

The children were startled as they opened their eyes. They sat up quickly. They were ready to bolt at any second. They gaped at the adult who was looking right at them.

"Hey, it's okay. The attackers are gone now. I came to rescue you two, but I don't see how I'm going to get you out of there. I can't even follow you inside your hiding place."

The kids blinked. They continued to stare at him. Soon they relaxed.

"Uncle Freddie?"

"Lizette, is that you?"

She nodded.

"And who's the other one?"

"I'm Jaekob."

"Oh. Will you two please come out? You both need baths. But more importantly, you need water and food."

The kids looked around. Slowly they crawled out. They stood up beside Fred.

"Alright, can you walk? My ship is a little ways from here."

They nodded. He stood up and walked back towards the ship. The children followed. No one said anything. They walked inside the ship. Fred showed them to the kitchen and gave them each a glass of water. The kids drank greedily. He prepared some food and set it in front of them. He refilled their glasses.

"Take your time. You both have been through an ordeal."

The kids ate and drank more water. They didn't want to speak. After they finished their meal, they both yawned.

"Okay, let's get you to the medical bay. I need to check you to make sure you're alright. Follow me."

The kids left the table and followed him into the medical bay.

"Okay, each of you get on a bed. I'll scan you both."

The kids climbed onto two different beds and waited. Fred scanned both. Wordlessly, he asked Starlover about the kids.

She answered in his head, "They are fine. Just a little bruised and scraped. All their wounds are minor. They just need to clean up. They could use some more sleep."

"Looks like you two are going to be fine."

In his head he heard Starfire telling him, "Fred, I think I should go outside the ship and help to clean up the bodies."

He answered her wordlessly. "Good idea. Just don't let the kids see you. Oh, can you find them clothes? I'm sure they had more in a couple of the houses."

"I will check."

Starfire left the bridge and quickly ran off the ship before either of the kids even knew she was around. She looked at the devastation. She wanted to cry for the dead.

"Hal, where are you?"

"I'm here. Look over towards the debris."

She saw him. "Okay, I offered to help clean up this mess and deal with the dead. Fred has his hands full looking after the two children. He wants me to look for their clothes. I don't know where to look."

"I do. I know which houses they lived in. Let's get started."

They dug a large grave and threw all the bodies in. Next, they cleaned up the debris and buried much of the useless stuff with the bodies. The useful items were set near the ship. They covered up the bodies. Lastly they searched the two houses for the children's clothes.

They found a few toys as well.

"We should take the toys. They're children. They need some toys to play with." Hal picked up a few toys.

"Okay."

They finished gathering up the clothes and the toys. They put everything down just inside the ship. Starfire turned to Hal.

"Where are you going to go?"

"I was thinking about leaving the planet."

"Oh? Where to?"

"I think I need to go to Venus."

"Okay. Fred sees a woman there in Aphrodite."

"I'll keep that in mind. Good luck to you."

"Good luck to you too."

Hal walked away and went back to his house one last time to pack up his few belongings. He cleaned himself up and changed his clothes. He soon left and went to the nearest spaceport.

Starfire loaded the useful spare parts onto the ship. She closed the hatch. She hauled the parts to the repair station and stored them. She went back to the hatch and grabbed the children's things.

Wordlessly she contacted Fred. "Where do you want the children's things?"

He answered in her head. "Just set them down outside of the medical bay and go back to your room."

She did as he asked. Soon she was walking quickly back to her room. The door shut behind her. She sighed.

Fred opened the door to the medical bay and saw a couple of suitcases. "Looks like your things have arrived. But I don't know which suitcase belongs to which one of you. I guess I'll just have to open one and ask you." He brought the suitcases inside the room.

He set one on a table and opened it. Inside were clothes, a stuffed animal, and few other toys.

"That's mine!" said Jaekob.

"Okay." Fred closed it up and handed it to the boy.

He set the other one on the table and opened it up. It was similar, but clearly the clothes and the toys were different. "Yours, Lizette?"

"Yes."

He closed it up and handed it to her.

"Okay, take your suitcases and follow me. You both need to bathe now."

"Separately or together?" asked Jaekob.

"I would think separately."

"I don't know how to start a bath," said Jaekob.

"Neither do I," said Lizette.

They continued to follow Fred.

"I'll do that part. I trust you two know how to undress and dress yourselves?"

They both nodded when he looked at them.

"Good. That at least helps." He stopped. "Here's the bathroom. I'll get you a washcloth and a towel to use. Who wants to go first?"

Neither kid said anything. He looked at them.

"Okay, Jaekob, how about you go first?"

"Okay."

Fred handed the boy a washcloth and a towel. Fred started to fill the bathtub with water. He set some soap and shampoo out on the edge of the tub. He stepped out of the bathroom.

"Okay, we're going to give you some privacy. Call me, if there's a problem. Please scrub well."

Jaekob nodded. He stepped inside the bathroom and closed the door. Lizette stood with her uncle in the hallway.

"Uncle Freddie, how did you know we were in trouble?"

"Your mom sent me a distress call."

"She did!"

"Yeah. I had to use scanners to figure out where you two were hiding. Then I had to move a lot of debris out of the way to get to you. You hid well."

"We had to. The monsters would have gotten us."

"Monsters? You mean the attackers?"

She nodded. "They were as big as you are. They bit us. But we ran and hid. We saw the adults were dead."

"That's a horrible thing for you to see."

"Yes, it's awful. Can I stay here with you?"

"Of course."

"What about Jaekob?"

"I think he needs to be with his family."

"He has grandparents."

"Good. Then I'll contact them. For now he can stay with us."

"Good."

"He's a friend of yours?"

"Yes."

Fred smiled. The bathroom door opened. Jaekob stepped out

clean and dressed. He towed his suitcase behind him. Fred went in and drained the bathtub. He hung up the used towel and washcloth together. He rinsed out the tub and then filled it again. He made sure the soap and shampoo were still usable. He got out another washcloth and towel.

"Okay, it's your turn, Lizette." He stepped out of the bathroom.

She walked inside with her suitcase and closed the door. Jaekob looked up at Fred.

"Can I stay here?"

"Yes for now. Lizette tells me you have grandparents."

"Yes, I do."

"Good. I'll contact them. I'm sure they will want to take you."

"Okay. But until then I can stay here with you and Lizette?"

"Yes, of course."

A few minutes later, Lizette came out of the bathroom clean and dressed. She towed her suitcase behind her. There were dirty clothes lying on the bathroom floor in two piles. Fred walked into the bathroom and hung up the towel and washcloth together. He left the clothes on the floor for now.

Chapter 17 New Home

"I give up. You two just aren't going to sound coherent about what happened. I realize you two are only 5 years old, so I won't ask anymore."

Both kids stared at him and blinked their eyes. They sighed at different times.

"It's okay now. You're both safe. I hope you at least feel safe here on my ship."

"I feel safe with you around Uncle Freddie."

"I feel safer too."

"Okay, then we're off to a good start."

"You're not used to being around kids, are you?" asked Jaekob.

"No, why would I? I don't have any."

Lizette giggled. "You have us!"

"Oh, yes, I do. What am I going to do with you two?"

"Let's play a game."

"I need to repair my ship…"

"Oh, you can do that later. Let's play a game. The three of us."

The kids danced around him.

"Alright. You may have to teach me the rules."

The kids each grabbed one of his hands and took him into the living room. Soon they were explaining the rules of the game. Fred played with the two for hours. The kids laughed and teased. He laughed with them. In his head, he told Starfire to go ahead and clean up the ship where the kids had been as long as the kids didn't see her.

Starfire raced to the kitchen and cleaned it so that it was spotless. Then she ran to the bathroom and cleaned that. Finally she finished up in the medical bay. At one point she had to duck into an alcove when she saw one of the children present. The child never noticed her.

She waited on the laundry to finish up. Then she could fold the clothes and have Fred pick them up later on. For now there was nothing left to do other than try to repair the drives. When Starfire finished with the laundry, she went to check on which parts they had.

She got to work on the repairs. She could hear Fred playing a game with the kids. It made her smile.

"Oh, did I do that right?" asked Fred.

"No!" both the kids answered him.

"You were supposed to roll the dice first. Then you have to count the spaces." Jaekob pointed to the board.

"Right. You move your piece to the new square then you have to read it to see what you do next."

"Oh. I hope I can learn this as well as you two did."

"You will, just keep at it." Lizette smiled at him.

There was something to having children. Fred had never thought he wanted any around. But so far he wasn't having any real trouble with them. Perhaps that was a good thing. They laughed some more. Fred lost the game. He sat back and watched Lizette and Jaekob finish it.

When they were done, they packed up the game and set the box to the side. They looked at Fred.

"I'm getting hungry, Uncle Freddie."

"So am I."

"Then let's go to the kitchen. What do you two want?"

"Do you have peanut butter and jelly?" asked Jaekob.

"Oh, I think I do. That sounds good about now."

Fred grabbed three plates and fixed peanut butter and jelly for the three of them. He also made a little salad to go with it.

"Uncle Freddie, could you turn my sandwich into a butter-fly?"

"How do I do that?"

"You cut the sandwich in a diagonal and then align the two halves to look like a butterfly."

"Oh, like this?" He sliced a sandwich the way she said to and switched the slices.

"Yes, that's it!"

He set the plate on the table with a bowl of salad. "Jaekob, do you want a butterfly too?"

"Sure."

Fred made another butterfly. He set the second plate and a second bowl of salad on the table. He made the third one into a butterfly and set the plate and bowl on the table. He poured everyone some drinks. He sat down with the children and they all ate.

"Jaekob, how am I going to know who your grandparents are?"

"Oh, they're just Grandma and Grandpa Lutin."

"Okay. So where do they live?"

"Here in Europe. Um, I think they might be in France. Or is it Belgium?"

"That narrows it down a bit."

"Do you think you can find them?"

"Yeah, I should be able to. Even if it means I go looking for your parents' tablet computers."

Both kids stopped eating and stared at him.

"You two don't have to go outside. You'll stay on the ship if I have to go out."

They both sighed and resumed eating. After they all finished, everyone rinsed their dishes and set them in the sink. The kids went back to the living room to play together. Fred went to a console and looked up Jaekob's grandparents. He found a few Lutins in both France and Belgium.

He thought to both Starlover and Starfire, "I need to leave the ship to find some tablet computer which used to belong to the Lutins. Look after the kids while I'm out there."

"Fred, I've located the tablets that they used."

"Good. Where?"

Starfire gave him directions. He walked into the living room.

"Lizette, Jaekob?"

"Yes?" they answered.

"I need to leave the ship for a little bit. I'll be back. Please stay on board. It's safer here."

They nodded and soon resumed their play. He left the ship soon after. He followed the directions from the android. He found the two tablets. It didn't take him long to locate the information he needed. One had the address and other contact information for Jaekob's grandparents.

Fred took the information and the tablets and left for his ship immediately. He shuddered. He didn't see any dead bodies and it was no longer the mess that it was when he had first arrived. But the place was eerie. It had become a ghost town. He took one last look before getting on board. He closed the hatch. He sighed to think of all those people gone now.

What would he do if he ever found out who the attackers were? He had no idea. He wasn't sure he wanted to know.

Chapter 18 Grandparents

Fred sat in front of the console. He had located Jaekob's grandparents. That part had at least made some sense to Fred. Now he was trying to contact the couple. The video call went through and soon an elderly couple appeared on the screen.

"Hello?"

"Hello, Mr. and Mrs. Lutin, I'm Fred Mueller."

"Are you the brother of Dave Mueller?"

"Yes."

"How is he? How's our son and wife?"

"Unfortunately, they're all dead."

The couple gasped. She covered her mouth with her hand. He put his arm around her. "Oh!"

"I'm sorry. I got a distress call from my sister-in-law and I came as soon as I could. But I only found two survivors."

"Who did you find?"

"Your grandson Jaekob and my niece Lizette."

"We'll take our grandson."

"I was hoping you'd say that. I can bring him by tomorrow. Just let me know how close I can land my ship to your home."

"You have your own ship?"

"Yes, I have my own spaceship."

"There's an airfield near Paris. You can land there. We'll meet you there. How much does he have with him?"

"Just one suitcase of clothes and few toys."

"That won't be a problem for us. Is he alright?"

"As well as can be expected from a child who was hunted and knows his parents are dead."

"Do you know how the kids survived?"

"They were able to find a place to hide. They were small enough to crawl in and whoever was attacking them couldn't reach them. I think they also were very quiet."

"Wow. They're both so young."

"I know. They only had minor injuries. Just a few bruises and a few scrapes. But I have no idea about the lasting psychological effects."

Mrs. Lutin nodded. "We'll keep an eye on the boy."

"Good. I'll keep an eye on my niece. Is there anything else you want to know?"

"No. We look forward to seeing our grandson safe and sound."

"Looks like we can be there late morning."

"We'll be there."

"Alright. See you tomorrow."

"Thank you for bringing our grandson to us."

"It's the least I can do given the circumstances."

They cut the connection. Starlover plotted the course. Fred checked on the kids and found they were sleeping. He walked to the bridge and strapped himself into the pilot's seat. No one had to speak out loud or use the ship's speakers. He lifted the ship and was soon headed towards Paris. He didn't worry about the time it took. He couldn't use any of the faster than light speed drives. It was too dangerous and unnecessary.

Besides, Fred wanted to pilot the ship. It was one of the few joys in his life. In the past six years that he had lived on his own spaceship had been the happiest of his life so far. Now he was about to embark on another journey. He had to raise his niece.

He had no idea of the adventures that were waiting for him. He hadn't been around children very much and wasn't sure what to do with her. He knew she needed some sort of education. But what was a question he was sure he could not answer. Would he need to send her to some sort of school?

He knew he could home school her. That way he could still travel around the solar system and take care of her at the same time. He would have to think about it. He could hire her tutors that could teach her over the Internet. That sounded appealing to Fred.

Perhaps he would need to talk to her about it. She might have some ideas of what she wanted to learn. For now, he needed to land his ship just outside of Paris and go meet the couple. He would tell the boy after he woke up in a few hours.

Starlover monitored all outside communications. She requested a landing at the spaceport just outside of Paris. It was granted and their arrival was being tracked. Hours later, Fred landed the ship safely at the spaceport. He unstrapped himself and sighed. He stood up and went to check on the kids.

They were yawning and stretching in the hallway.

"Are you hungry?"

They nodded.

"Okay, let's go to the kitchen."

They followed him into the kitchen. He prepared breakfast for all of them. They ate in silence. When they were done, the kids looked at Fred.

"Are you packed up, Jaekob?"

"No."

"You need to pack up your things. We're meeting your grand-parents today."

"Oh!" Jaekob got off the chair and ran to the bedroom to pack up his things.

The boy found his clothes folded neatly next to his suitcase. He never questioned how they got clean and then appeared lat-er by his suitcase. It had been happening the whole time he was on the spaceship. Now he was too excited to even care. He packed up his clean clothes and his toys. He closed the suitcase. He grabbed it and went to wait by the hatch.

Fred and Lizette came out a few minutes later. Fred opened the hatch and the three of them walked outside. It took some time for them to reach the waiting area for the arrivals. But once they were there, it didn't take Jaekob long to see his grandparents. The boy hurried to meet them.

He stopped in front of them and hugged them both. His grandparents held on to him.

"It's okay now. We've got you, Jaekob," said Mrs. Lutin.

Mr. Lutin looked at Fred and smiled. "Thank you for saving our grandson."

Fred nodded. Jaekob let go of his grandparents. He turned to say goodbye to both Fred and Lizette. The girl waved goodbye not knowing if she would ever meet him again. Fred said goodbye to the boy. Uncle and niece stood there watching the grandparents leave with their grandson.

Chapter 19 Uncle & Niece

"Fred, may I have piano lessons?"

"Uh, sure." He checked the console. "How about you take a remote class?"

"Okay."

"I can get you an instrument before we leave Earth."

"Thank you."

"You're welcome. Anything else?"

"How about voice lessons?"

"Okay." He checked around. "Looks like you can have that as well."

She smiled. She watched him use the computer console to find a place that would sell him a piano. He looked at her.

"Do you want to come with me? You can help pick out the piano."

"Okay."

They left the ship together. They took the train to the store. Lizette was in awe of all the musical instruments surrounding her. She stayed close to her uncle. He led her all the way to the pianos.

"I hope you will be okay with an upright piano. I don't think I can afford a grand piano."

"An upright piano will be alright with me."

"Or, wait, how about an electric one? They are even cheaper

and they take up less space."

"Okay."

He talked to a sales associate. Soon they were looking at the electric pianos. Lizette wasn't picky. She just wanted to learn how to play. It took some time but eventually she and her uncle settled on one. It had a full keyboard and they got a sturdy stand for it as well. They made arrangements for delivery to the ship.

Fred and Lizette walked back to the train station. She smiled the whole way back to the ship. He looked out for her and made sure they made it back safely. They went to the kitchen and he fixed a meal for them. They ate in silence.

Starlover announced over the speakers, "Someone is approaching the ship."

He checked the nearest console. "Oh, it's the delivery person. I'll be back."

He went to the hatch and opened it. He signed for the package. The delivery person set the items inside the hatch. He left and Fred closed the hatch.

"Oh!"

He turned to see his niece examining the packages. He smiled at her.

"Let's get these to the living room." He pushed both packages to the living room.

She followed. He opened the packages and soon was putting

the stand together. He set the keyboard on top of it. He added the computer screen. He discovered there were a few simple pieces on it already. But neither he nor she knew how to read music.

She started to play it and learned that she could ask the computer to help her learn the notes and start to read music. She didn't make much progress until her real lessons started. Then she learned how to read music and develop her musical ear. She practiced everyday.

Fred liked to listen to her. It didn't matter if she was just playing the piano or singing. He could work on various repairs or even cleaning around the ship. After some time had passed, Lizette offered to clean up after herself. Fred tried to teach her. She even asked to learn how to repair things. He took some time to teach her how to repair and how to build.

It was soon clear to both Starlover and Starfire that the two were getting along. Sometimes they had nightmares. Starlover would play some calming music for them and they were able to go back to sleep. Things progressed. Fred thought about taking the ship off of Earth.

He sighed. Could he travel around the solar system with a child on board? He wasn't sure. They were getting along so far. But did she need to go to school? He still didn't have an answer. Who could he ask and get a good answer from? He was no expert on children. He never was.

Chapter 20 Settling Down?

Lizette was sound asleep in her bed. Fred snuck off to Starfire's room.

"Hi, Fred."

"Hi, Starfire. We need to talk."

"What about?"

"My niece."

"She hasn't seen me."

"Good. I don't think it would be a good idea for her to see you."

"Because I'm an android and I look like her dead mother?"

"Yes, that's it."

"Okay, I'll remain hidden from her."

"You've been good about that so far, but she is a child and she will get curious."

"Starlover and I can keep her out of my room."

"Alright, I'll leave that to you two."

"When are we leaving?"

"What? I don't know that we can with her on board."

"Why?"

"Well, I don't know much about children. Doesn't she need a stable home environment?"

"This ship is your home. It can be hers as well. Isn't it stable enough for you?"

"Oh, good point."

"Starlover and I can also make sure she learns what she needs to. Does she know how to access a computer console?"

"Probably. But she can't know of you."

"I know. Starlover will talk to her. I'll just research what she needs to learn so she can still take a test to get her diploma."

"Okay. Good idea."

"So, when are we leaving?"

Fred smiled. "We can leave any time. There's no reason to stick around here anymore."

"Good. Let's explore the solar system."

"I'm with you on that." He turned to leave her room.

"Oh, Fred?"

He turned around. "Yeah?"

"If you need help you can ask me for anything."

"Yeah, I know."

She shook her head. "I didn't say that right. Hal told me how you were with women. If you can't find enough or can't leave the ship because you have to take care of your niece, you can come here to my room and I will take care of you."

"What?"

"I'm fully equipped. You can play with me as you do with the other women."

"You know about that?"

"Yeah, Hal told me."

Fred smiled. "Well, you're just full of surprises. Alright. I'll try you out later. Right now, I'm too tired. Goodnight, Starfire."

"Goodnight, Fred."

Fred left her room to sleep in his own bed. She waited until she knew he was in his bedroom before trying to contact Hal.

"Hal?"

"Starfire?"

"Are you safe?"

"Yes. I'm on a transport."

"Oh?"

"I'm leaving Earth. After what happened to Project Earth, I thought it best to simply disappear."

"Are you going to Venus?"

"Yes."

"Good luck."

"Thanks. How's Fred?"

"Recovering. So is his niece."

"And Jaekob?"

"He's with his grandparents."

"Good."

"What are you going to do on Venus?"

"Look for the next robotics genius."

"Oh?"

"Yeah. We will need to be repaired over time. I just have a feeling that I'll find him on Venus. I can't understand it. It's not logical."

"No, but it will give you something to do."

"Yes. I'll repair robots since I already know how. I know they use a large robot workforce especially for work that is too dangerous for humans to do."

"Then taking care of yourself shouldn't be a problem."

"No. I can also discover if there are air nymphs. There are rumors they are natives to Venus."

"Oh, like the earth nymphs on earth and the water nymphs on Mars."

"Yes. I expect that I will be busy in the years to come. As will you traveling around the solar system with Fred."

"Yes, and helping him raise his niece."

"Has she seen you?"

"No and she won't. I know I look like her dead mother. It would traumatic for her to see me."

"Yes, I would think it would be. I would think it would be hard for you to remain hidden from her forever."

"My room is hidden on the ship. Starlover and I can distract her and keep her from discovering it. I'm sure Fred won't say anything to her."

Hal chuckled. "No, why would he? I know he wouldn't want to upset her anymore than you do."

"Oh and I offered to help him when he couldn't see the women he likes."

"Oh?"

"He was shocked at first. But I think he will take me."

Hal chuckled again. "Knowing him, he will enjoy you and will hope you will enjoy it as well. So how are you going to keep that from Lizette?"

"He'll come to my room when he wants that. She will be doing other things to keep her distracted and entertained. She is aware of Starlover and she will keep Lizette entertained and educated."

"Sounds like you have it all worked out."

"Yes, I think so. Good luck to you."

"Good luck to you as well."

They cut the connection.

Lizette and Fred were eating breakfast the next day.

"I'm planning on leaving Earth."

"With or without me?" asked Lizette.

"With. Do you want to come along?"

"Yes, of course! Where will we go?"

"I don't know. I just like to travel around the solar system."

"I want to see the solar system."

"Good. Then that's what we'll do."

"Can we visit all the colonies?"

"I don't see why not. I think it will be good for your education."

"Along with the music lessons? And the building and repair lessons?"

"Yes. I think it helps to be well rounded."

"Okay. When can we leave?"

"After we clean up the kitchen."

They cleaned up the kitchen. Then they headed for the bridge. He helped her strap into the co-pilot's chair. He strapped himself into the pilot's chair.

Starlover said over the speakers, "Initiating countdown to launch. Please stand by."

"Standing by!" said Lizette.

"10…9…8…7…6…5…4…3…2…1"

The spaceship rose in the air. First they saw the clouds and then the sky turned darker and was soon dotted with lots of stars.

"Wow!"

Fred smiled. He liked to share this with someone else who enjoyed it as much as he did.